STERLING CHILDREN'S BOOKS
New York

An Imprint of Sterling Publishing Co., Inc.
1166 Avenue of the Americas
New York, NY 10036

ISBN 978-1-4549-1946-9

Distributed in Canada by Sterling Publishing Co., Inc.
c/o Canadian Manda Group, 664 Annette Street
Toronto, Ontario, Canada M6S 2C8
Distributed in the United Kingdom by GMC Distribution Services
Castle Place, 166 High Street, Lewes, East Sussex, England BN7 1XU
Distributed in Australia by NewSouth Books
45 Beach Street, Coogee, NSW 2034, Australia

For information about custom editions, special sales, and premium and corporate purchases,
please contact Sterling Special Sales at 800-805-5489 or specialsales@sterlingpublishing.com.

Manufactured in China

Lot #:
1 2 3 4 5 6 7 8 9 10
03/17

www.sterlingpublishing.com

The artwork for this book was created digitally.
Designed by Heather Kelly

To Hedy Bohm, and in memory
of her father and mother, Ignac and
Erzsebet (née Breuer) Klein. —C. M.

To Emi, the most fanatic
of pizza lovers. —E. S.

WORLD PIZZA

BY CECE MENG

ILLUSTRATED BY ELLEN SHI

STERLING CHILDREN'S BOOKS

New York

The tall hill with the cherry trees and the soft grass for chairs was the best place to look for a wishing star. Mama found such a star, the first to be seen in more than one hundred years. It was not the brightest nor the biggest in the sky that night, but it was still a true wishing star. So Mama made her wish.

"I wish for world peace—ah . . . ahh . . . ahh-*CHOO!*" said Mama. A floating cherry blossom had tickled her nose into a giant sneeze.

"Mama wished for world pizza!" said Jack.

"I think she meant world peace," said Papa.

"I definitely heard world pizza," said Joe.

"*Peace*," said Papa.

"PIZZA!" howled baby Moe. He reached up and squeezed Papa's nose.

"Let's not fight," said Mama.

Just then, a pizza fell from the sky, landing gentle as a warm blanket on Mama's lap. The kids didn't know about peace, but they knew about pizza. And this particular pizza was delicious.

Mama, in her heart, still wished for peace, for a world filled with kindness and love and no fighting. But she agreed, the pizza was delicious. So they ate until their bellies were full and everyone was happy.

Across the world in another town, on another hill, sat another family. And another pizza, carried on the wind, appeared. This one landed atop the father's head.

That family agreed the pizza was delicious. So they ate until their bellies were full and everyone was happy.

Pizza appeared in valleys, in deserts, and on the very topmost points of snowy, blowy mountains.

Pizza rained down onto cars,
subways, boats, and planes.

People living in the
biggest building of the
biggest town got pizza.

People living in the smallest building of the smallest town got pizza.

People with no place to live at all got pizza. (Those people got *extra* pizza.)

There was spicy pepper pizza, salty seaweed pizza, chocolate cherry pizza, and extra-cheesy-with-pickles pizza. None of the pizzas were the same, but they were all delicious.

Some people dipped their pizza in hummus, while others dipped their pizza in guacamole. Some people made pizza chow mein and some people made pizza sushi. Some even made pizza soup. They all agreed the different pizzas were delicious. So they shared and everyone was happy.

The bully on the playground pointed and laughed at the unusual looking pizzas until the kids offered him slices.

He ate and realized he liked the new flavors, and he liked his new friends even more.

The pirates on the rough ocean seas put down their swords to eat pizza.

They agreed the pizza was superb. Once they stopped fighting, they realized they were tired of being angry and tired of hurting each other, so they kicked their swords to the bottom of the sea. And all the pirates were happy.

Even angry neighbors with tall fences and locked doors got pizza.
They peeked over their fences and frowned at the pizzas that looked
nothing like their own.

They shook their fists and called out "GO AWAY!" until the scrumptious smell made them stop, and they looked at the faces of all the different people eating every kind of pizza imaginable.

They saw the smiles and they couldn't help but smile back.
So they opened their doors wide and joined the fun outside.

There were pizza-tossing contests.

There were pizza parties.

There was even a pizza parade.

People all over the world talked and laughed and ate until their bellies were full. Even after the pizza was gone, the people stayed. They made friends.

And in that moment the world was filled with kindness and love and no fighting.

On top of the tall hill with the cherry trees and the soft grass for chairs, Mama picked up the last piece of pizza. She gave it to the stray dog that followed them home.

As Mama tucked Jack, Joe, and baby Moe into bed, Jack yawned and said, "Mama, I'm sorry you didn't get your wish for world peace."

Mama gave each child a kiss and turned out the light. "Next time," she whispered.

The family fell asleep, cozy in the warmth of their peaceful dreams.

And everyone was happy.

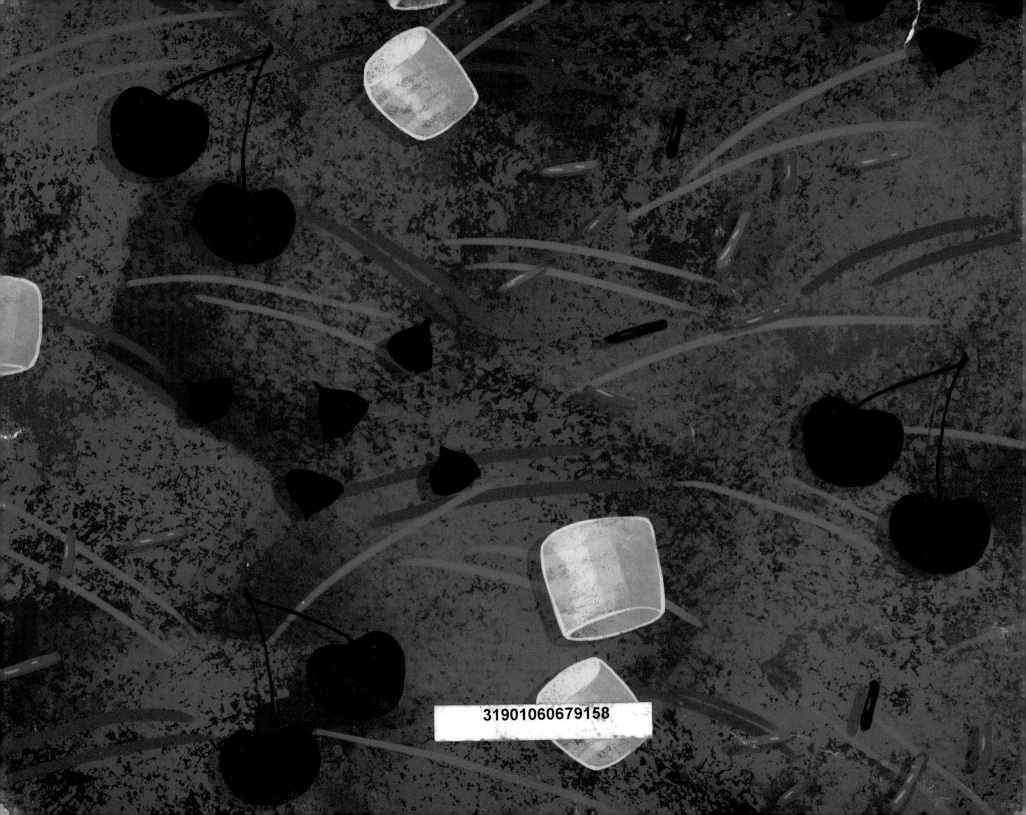